First U.S. edition 1993
First published in Great Britain in 1992
by Walker Books Ltd., London.

Library of Congress Cataloging-in-Publication Data:

Oxenbury, Helen.
Tom and Pippo on the beach / Helen Oxenbury.

Summary : Tom and his stuffed monkey Pippo trade sun
hats when they go to the beach with Daddy.
[1. Toys—Fiction. 2. Beaches—Fiction.] I. Title.
PZ7.0975Tqg   1993   92-53130   [E]—dc20
ISBN 1-56402-181-5

10 9 8 7 6 5 4 3 2 1

Printed in Hong Kong

The pictures in this book were done
in watercolor and pencil line.

Candlewick Press
2067 Massachusetts Avenue
Cambridge, Massachusetts 02140

TOM and PIPPO
on the beach

Helen Oxenbury

CANDLEWICK PRESS
CAMBRIDGE, MASSACHUSETTS

One day Daddy and I
went to the beach in the car…

and of course Pippo
came too.

Daddy said that the
sun was really bright
and that I should wear my
hat, because the sun
might make me sick.

I said that it didn't seem
bright to me and I didn't
feel sick and anyway Pippo
needed to wear my hat.

Daddy said he would make a hat for Pippo so that I could wear my hat. He said he would make Pippo a hat out of newspaper.

I said to Daddy,
"Look, Pippo doesn't
like the paper hat."

"I know! I'll wear it
and he can wear mine."

I'm glad Pippo's got the best hat, so he won't feel sick in the sun.